The Adventure

NINJA and LUCHE

The Great Piggy Rescue

Written by: Josh Eagan
Illustrated by: Ani Eagan

For more information, please contact:
MoFat Publishing
PO BOX 4484
Roanoke, VA 24015
Ninja@ninjaandluche.com
Luche@ninjaandluche.com

Library of Congress Control Number: 2019913239

ISBN 978-0-578-56944-4

Thank you to Anika and Evelyn for introducing me to the wonderful world of Ninja and Luche. Without their creativeness, the world would have never met these characters.

Special thanks to my wife, Andrea, who allowed Ninja and Luche to visit us so often over the past six years.
- Josh Eagan

Thanks to my sister for always inspiring me to be creative and silly. - Ani Eagan

It was the first day of summer break. Monica and her brother Stevie were already planning for the adventures that were about to begin.

Mom's voice came from downstairs.

"Kids, it's time for breakfast... Come on down!"

"Let's go, Stevie. We have to get to breakfast—put away that cape!" Monica said as she hung up her own costume.

Stevie reluctantly listened to his big sister and walked down the steps to the kitchen.

"What are you two going to do on your first day of summer break?" Mom asked while she got herself ready for work.

"Don't forget, Grandma will be by around noon to fix you lunch and make sure everything is going all right," Dad explained as he was rushing out the door. "I'll leave you some money on the counter in case you need anything."

"Not yet, Stevie—we have to stick to our plan," Monica replied with just as much excitement. "Wait until they get to the end of the street."

"Okay, now!" Monica shouted, but as she turned, she saw Stevie already running up the stairs. "STEVIE, you were supposed to wait!"

In their room, Monica opened her tablet and started to search frantically.

"Do you have anything, Monica? Can I put on my costume?" Stevie asked as he jumped on the bed.

"Hold on, I think we got a new request for help . . . yep, we did!" said Monica with a huge smile. "Do you know that little girl named Joy from our school? She had her favorite stuffed animal taken away from her. She needs us to get it back."

Monica turned to her brother. "Suit up, Stevie . . ."

As Ninja and Luche walked through town to get to Joy's house, Luche waved to his fans and posed for pictures.

"Luche, be SNEAKY like a ninja!" exclaimed Ninja, ducking behind a tree.

"These people love us, Ninja—how can I be sneaky at a time like this?" Luche said as he signed an autograph for a child who didn't ask for one.

"Oooh, nachos!" Luche screamed, running toward a taco stand.

"Stevie—I mean Luche—we need to go! No nachos!"

When Ninja and Luche arrived at Joy's house, she explained to the heroes what had happened.

". . . and now James has Piggy," Joy sobbed.

"Not to worry, Joy, we're really sneaky," said Ninja. "We'll get Piggy back, right Luche? . . . Luche??"

"Mmm . . . Right, Ninja," Luche agreed, trying to hide the nacho cheese that was dripping from his mask.

Ninja looked over at Luche in disbelief. "How did you even get those nachos? Oh, never mind. We have a job to do—but first, can I have some nachos?

While Ninja, Luche, and Joy were enjoying the delicious, cheesy nachos together, they saw James on his porch with Piggy.

Ninja and Luche started working on a plan to get Piggy back in Joy's hands.

"The key is we need to be SNEAKY!" Ninja loudly explained.

"I'll fly in while you distract him with your ninja dance moves," Luche said through a mouthful of tortilla chips. "Then we'll give him the cake!"

Quietly, Ninja and Luche sneaked into James' yard. The heroes' plan was going well until . . .

"NINJA!!" Ninja yelled as she ran up to James, being anything but sneaky.

"Ninja dance party time!"

James' eyes flew open wide.

"Ya-ya-ya, do the Ninja, hey-ya," sang Ninja as a confused James watched.

"Dance with Ninja, James!"

As Ninja grabbed James to show him the ninja moves, James looked up and saw Luche, who was making his less than sneaky and graceful entrance.

Luche attempted to fly into the yard to make his heroic introduction. "This is a job for the one and only Luch-ahhhh!!!" The intro was cut short when he tripped on his own costume and rolled to James' feet.

"Be more SNEAKY!" Ninja screamed as she continued to dance.

"Um . . . who are you guys?" James asked, baffled—and a bit entertained.

"We're Ninja and Luche. You haven't heard of us? We're kind of a big deal," explained Ninja.

Luche ran up and interrupted, "We heard it was your birthday, so we brought you a delicious, special cake."

"What kind of cake is that? And what is a 'Luche'?" asked James as he peered at the slice of cake.

"It's a special surprise cake for your birthday, made using our Secret Luche Recipe," explained Luche.

"But my birthday isn't for another three months," James groaned.

"JUST EAT THE CAKE!" Ninja yelled, and Luche took Piggy away from James and quickly gave him the piece of cake.

"Well . . . I do love cake, and this looks delicious," James said with a smile. He moved it toward his mouth to take a bite.

"Luche, watch out!" Ninja shouted.

The heroes bolted away as the cake exploded. As they fled, Luche again tripped and fell— gracefully.

"My cake! What happened to my cake?" James cried out, wiping cake splatters from his eyes. He wrinkled his nose. "Hey, this isn't even icing—it's shaving cream."

Ninja and Luche laughed hysterically as they ran back to Joy's house.

Joy was so happy when she saw Piggy in Ninja's hands.

"Thank you, Ninja and Luche! You saved Piggy and made my day. You guys are heroes!"

"Let's celebrate with our ninja dance," an excited Ninja suggested. "Piggy can dance too!"

But their celebration was cut short when Luche looked at the time.

"Holy Lucha libre. We're going to be late! Ninja, we have to go. Stop dancing . . . NINJA!!!"

"Thanks Ninja and Luche!" Joy said excitedly. "I'm going to go check on James. He did take Piggy, but he's a nice kid. Maybe we can play with Piggy together."

Ninja snapped to attention and the two heroes dashed out of Joy's yard.

"Thanks again, Ninja and Luche," Joy shouted, waving to her heroes.

On the way home, Luche again got distracted by his fans. He bounded up to people, offering to take selfies with them and giving them his autograph without being asked.

"Luche, enough with the selfies. We have to get home now," Ninja said. She continued to walk, watching Luche scribble his signature on a dog's collar.

"Ninja, we're almost home! We're going to make it before Grandma gets there," Luche exclaimed. Running ahead of Ninja, he turned the corner and called back, "Bet I can beat you."

But as Ninja got to the corner, she saw their neighbor, Mr. Picklebob, outside getting his mail. "Luche, he's going to see us—slow down!" she yelled. "We can't let him see us go into our house."

But it was too late. Mr. Picklebob was at his mailbox and turning to look their way.

Mr. Picklebob caught sight of Ninja and Luche.

"Who the heck are you guys?" he grumbled. "Why are you in front of my house? You need to get off my lawn."

Ninja panicked. She did not want their secret superhero identity to be found out.

Ninja stumbled on her words. "Um, well, Mr. Picklebob . . ."

"Don't worry, Ninja, I got this," said Luche.

"We are agents Ninja and Luche from Animal Control. Your dog O'Brian has been seen FLYING around the neighborhood. Have you seen her recently?" Luche asked confidently.

Ninja looked at Luche and whispered, "Really, Luche? That's your plan? A flying dog?"

But to her surprise, it worked.

"Oh no! O'Brian!" Picklebob yelled as he started frantically looking around his yard for his dog.

"I can't believe that worked!" Ninja exclaimed as she and Luche began to run the other way.

"It worked, Ninja, but now we have another problem. RUN!" Luche screamed. Picklebob's dog O'Brian had heard her name, and now she came running. Her eyes were set on the strangers in her yard.

Ninja and Luche burst through their back door and were greeted by their own dog, Jack.

"Hiya boy! We can't pet you now—we have to get upstairs," said Monica as she pulled off her mask.

"Hey Ninja, why does Jack have my cape?" Luche asked as he ran up the stairs.

"I don't know, Stevie. Can you grab it from him?" said Monica as she put her costume away.

From downstairs, they heard their grandmother call out, "Monica, Stevie—where are you guys? I brought lunch."

Monica and Stevie ran down the stairs and greeted their grandma. "Hey, Grammy!" the kids screamed in unison.

"Are you guys doing okay? Not getting into any trouble today, right?" asked Grandma with a grin.

"Oh Grammy, of course not," Stevie laughed. "Just playing our new video game, The Adventures of Ninja and Luche."

"You should be outside in the fresh air," said Grandma. "Come on, let's go for a walk. I think Mr. Picklebob needs help finding his dog."

Stevie and Monica walked with their grandma, talking about their summer plans. They passed by Joy and Piggy; Joy was dancing with her favorite stuffed friend and singing the Ninja theme song she'd learned earlier.

"Look at that girl," Grandma said. "She looks so happy to have that stuffed animal. It must be really special to her."

"Yeah, Piggy sure is special, Grammy," Stevie said.

Grandma looked at Stevie, confused. "How do you know the stuffed animal's name, Stevie?"

Monica interrupted, "Oh, that's Joy—she goes to our school. She talks about Piggy all the time. And after all, every stuffed animal is special!"

About the Author

Josh Eagan is the owner and publisher of Roanoke Valley Family Magazine. He is married to his high school sweetheart, Andrea, who is a nurse at a local hospital. They have two kids, Anika and Evelyn, who are the creative forces behind Ninja and Luche. In his spare time, Josh can be found at the gym, watching baseball or simply just hanging out and playing with his family.

About the Illustrator

Anika Eagan is a student at Community High School in Roanoke, Virginia. She has been drawing and creating since she was five. Anika loves animals and volunteers at the local shelter when she is not busy at school or drawing the next *Ninja and Luche* book. Anika and her sister Evelyn can often be found baking in the kitchen, creating something in the basement or playing with their dogs, Bauer and Chloe.

Want more of NINJA & LUCHE

Go to: www.ninjaandluche.com

Made in the USA
Middletown, DE
28 March 2020